Red Shed

Illustrated by The Artful Doodlers

Random House New York
Thomas the Tank Engine & Friends™

CREATED BY BRITT ALLCROFT

Based on The Railway Series by The Reverend W Awdry. © 2010 Gullane (Thomas) LLC.
Thomas the Tank Engine & Friends and Thomas & Friends are trademarks of Gullane (Thomas) Limited.
HIT and the HIT Entertainment logo are trademarks of HIT Entertainment Limited.

www.stepintoreading.com   www.randomhouse.com/kids   www.thomasandfriends.com

Educators and librarians, for a variety of teaching tools, visit us at
www.randomhouse.com/teachers

ISBN: 978-0-375-85368-5   MANUFACTURED IN CHINA

Thomas.

Shed.

That shed is red.

Sled!

Can Thomas get that sled?

Thomas can get that sled!

Ten bells!

Can Thomas get the bells?

Thomas can get the bells!

Balls.

Can Thomas get the balls?

The men fell!

What a mess!

Thomas can not get the balls.

Kids!

The kids can get the balls.

Thomas gets the toys.

He can go.